Catkin Farm

ORCHARD BOOKS

Freddy, the farm cat, padded quietly across the moonlit fields, but something hideous barred his way.

It grinned at him with twisted teeth and popping eyes…

Like a bullet from a gun, Freddy
shot off through the wheat.

He burst into the secret circle of the
Scaredy Cats. Eight pairs of yellow
eyes gawped at his terrified face.

"It's i-i-i-in the b-b-big meadow!" he stammered. "I-i-it was trying to get me! Yellow eyes! Big t-t-teeth!"

The cats in the circle laughed.

"We've all seen it," said Fifi. "It's the new scarecrow!"

"Nothing to be scared of," said Purdy.

"Unless," growled Kipling, their leader, "it was a living scarecrow!"

Silence fell upon the secret circle.
Kipling's eyes narrowed into slits. He
was ready to tell a story. The story
they had all come to hear.

"Once," Kipling began, "I was young and very foolish. My brother, Nibs, and I loved to go hunting."

"We would visit Catkin Farm because the fields were full of mice and rats."

A rotten old scarecrow stood lonely in the fields. It didn't scare anyone!

No one lived at the farm. It was overgrown and the house was falling apart. Nibs and I treated the place as if it was our own.

One night, we were hunting in the
fields when we saw a light burning in
the window of the farmhouse.

Like moths drawn to a flame, Nibs
and I crept towards the house, quiet as
quiet could be.

As we jumped up to peer through
the dusty window, I felt my fur stand on
end, and my skin crawl with goose flesh.

A candle flickered in the kitchen,
illuminating an uneaten meal on the
table. A shadow appeared behind us.

Something grabbed us by the scruff of our necks and hissed in our ears. "If you ever come sneaking round here again, you'll be very, very sorry."

We bit, wriggled, scratched and tore
ourselves from its grasp. As we ran, I
looked back only once. It was enough.

A hideous face glowed in the
torchlight. It laughed like a wretched
old crow!

So Catkin Farm had a new owner. Mr Cawber was his name. He kept to the shadows. We never got a really good look at him.

"Keep Out" signs appeared all around the farm. Nibs and I didn't need to be told to stay away. But we wondered what was so secret. What was Mr Cawber hiding on his farm?

One day, an ambulance screamed
through the village. Mr Cawber had
appendicitis. He would have to stay in
hospital until he was well again.

I wasn't sorry. I'd had an excellent idea. While Mr Cawber was away, Nibs and I were going to play!

That night we squeezed through the new wire fence. The corn was high and dry. The dry leaves swished at us as we crept towards the house.

It was hard to be quiet. An eerie silence surrounded us. The fields used to be full of mice and rats scurrying about. Now, not even an insect twitched.

There would be no hunting. What had Mr Cawber done with all the wildlife?

The house was in darkness.
Moonlight cast strange shadows across
the porch. It almost looked as if...

Nibs nudged my paw. "It's him!" he croaked. My heart stopped. For a moment, ice ran through my veins. Mr Cawber sat on the porch, asleep in the rocking chair.

A cloud drifted in front of the moon.
When it passed, the shadows shifted.

Huh! It wasn't Mr Cawber at all,
but the rotten old scarecrow of
Catkin Farm!

Nibs laughed nervously. The scarecrow rocked gently in the chair. The stuffing rustled quietly inside its sack body.

The clouds shifted again and the face of the scarecrow was bathed in moonlight. "It does look just like him," I said nervously.

Nibs picked up a stick and jabbed the lifeless scarecrow in its tummy. "It's just a bag of stuffing," he said.

The sackcloth body twitched and let out an eerie, mournful sigh.

Ooooosh!

My throat tightened. I couldn't shout
a warning. The scarecrow's wooden
head moved silently. Its painted eyes
opened wide and stared at Nibs.

Nibs hadn't noticed. He poked the scarecrow again. This time the body jerked and sprang to life!

Did I see puppet strings? I don't know...I didn't stop to look.

We yowled and ran for our lives.

As we raced through the corn, leaves grabbed our paws, and cobs slammed in our faces. Finally we crashed into the fence.

We scrambled through the wire and never stopped running until we were home and safely tucked up in our warm beds.

We saw Mr Cawber later, when he was home from hospital. He was fixing the farm gate as we strolled by. We froze, rooted to the path.

His dark, shadowed eyes bore into us, like laser beams. His mouth twitched in a sly grin. He knew we'd been to the farm!

His voice was dry and rasping.
"What's the matter, boys? Has
something scared you?"

No doubt about it…he knew!

He laughed — a horrid, sickening
cackle — then he shuffled back down
the lane to his secret, sinister life at
Catkin Farm.

I don't need to tell you that Nibs
and I never, ever went there again."

The Secret Circle sat in hushed
silence as Kipling finished his story.

A familiar voice called across the still, night air. "Freddy! Freddy!"

"They're calling me," Freddy shivered. "I think I'll go the long way back home tonight. I don't want to meet any living scarecrows!"

The other cats laughed. They weren't afraid of living scarecrows. There were no such things... Or were there?

SCAREDY CATS

Shoo Rayner

❏ Frankatstein	1 84362 729 9	£3.99
❏ Foggy Moggy Inn	1 84362 730 2	£3.99
❏ Catula	1 84362 731 0	£3.99
❏ Catkin Farm	1 84362 732 9	£3.99
❏ Bluebeard's Cat	1 84362 733 7	£3.99
❏ The Killer Catflap	1 84362 744 2	£3.99
❏ Dr Catkyll and Mr Hyde	1 84362 745 0	£3.99
❏ Catnapped	1 84362 746 9	£3.99

Little HORRORS

❏ The Swamp Man	1 84121 646 1	£3.99
❏ The Pumpkin Man	1 84121 644 5	£3.99
❏ The Spider Man	1 84121 648 8	£3.99
❏ The Sand Man	1 84121 650 X	£3.99
❏ The Shadow Man	1 84362 021 X	£3.99
❏ The Bone Man	1 84362 010 3	£3.99
❏ The Snow Man	1 84362 009 X	£3.99
❏ The Bogey Man	1 84362 011 1	£3.99

These books are available from all good bookshops,
or can be ordered direct from the publisher:
Orchard Books, PO BOX 29, Douglas IM99 1BQ
Credit card orders please telephone 01624 836000 or fax 01624 837033
or e-mail: bookshop@enterprise.net for details.

To order please quote title, author and ISBN and your full name and address.
Cheques and postal orders should be made payable to 'Bookpost plc'.
Postage and packing is FREE within the UK
(overseas customers should add £1.00 per book).

Prices and availability are subject to change.